Sommer-Time Stories—Classics

Sommer's lively retelling of this classic Aesop fable.

The BOY Who Cried WOLF!

Retold by Carl Sommer
Illustrated by Enache Bogdan

First Edition

Library of Congress Cataloging-in-Publication Data

Sommer, Carl, 1930-
  The boy who cried wolf! / retold by Carl Sommer ; illustrated by Enache Bogdan. -- First edition.
    1 online resource. -- (Sommer-time stories-classics)
  Summary: "Nicholas has the world's most boring job-watching sheep. When he tries to liven up his chore with practical jokes, he loses peoples' trust. Nicholas realizes his mistake when the wolf attacks and everyone refuses to respond to his cry for help"-- Provided by publisher.
  Description based on print version record and CIP data provided by publisher; resource not viewed.
  ISBN 978-1-57537-079-8 (library binding : alk. paper) (print) -- ISBN 978-1-57537-441-3 (epub)
  ISBN 978-1-57537-479-6 (kf8) – ISBN 978-1-57537-492-5 (pdf)
  [1. Fables. 2. Folklore.] I. Bogdan, Enache, illustrator. II. Aesop. III. Title.
  PZ8.2.S635
  398.2--dc23
  [E]
                                    2013003324

Advance
PUBLISHING

"Take the sheep up to the hill where there's lots of green grass for them to eat," Dad said. "And don't forget that in the nearby forest lives a big wolf that loves to eat sheep. So always be careful to watch the sheep."

"I'll be careful," promised Nicholas.

Sometimes in the large forest it became hard for the big wolf to catch something to eat. When that happened, he took a chance to capture his favorite meal, a sheep.

Nicholas always had to be very careful that the wolf did not attack his sheep.

"I know watching sheep is important," Nicholas said to himself, "but it gets so boring. What can I do?"

Nicholas picked up a stone and threw it towards a tree. "That's a lot more fun than just sitting here watching sheep."

Nicholas spent hours throwing stones at trees and rocks.

Nicholas grew tired of throwing stones. "I'm bored," he groaned. "What else can I do?"

He sat under a shade tree and thought and thought. Suddenly an idea flashed through his mind. He jumped up and exclaimed, "I'll make a slingshot! That should be lots of fun!"

Nicholas sat down on a rock and made a slingshot.

Then Nicholas picked up stones and shot them with his slingshot against trees and rocks. "That's a lot more fun than just throwing stones," he said.

Soon his arm became tired. Nicholas sat down and wondered, "What else can I do? Shooting stones with a slingshot also gets boring."

Suddenly he jumped up and exclaimed, "I've got a great idea to have a little fun! I'll stand on a rock where everyone can see me, wave my hat, and yell, 'Wolf! Wolf!' Then the townspeople will

race up the hill to help me."

Nicholas let out a loud laugh. "Ha! Ha! Ha! It will be so funny to see everyone running, slipping, and falling as they dash up the hill."

Without thinking any further, Nicholas jumped on a rock, waved his hat, and cried as loud as he could, "Wolf! Wolf!"

Everyone heard Nicholas yelling, "Wolf! Wolf!"
Farmers left their horses in the field, women
stopped their washing, store owners left their
shops, and carpenters threw down their tools.
Everyone in town ran up the hill as fast as they

could go.

Nicholas hid behind a rock and laughed as he watched the townspeople slip, slide, and fall as they raced up the hill. "This is so, so funny!" he said. "I've never seen anything so funny."

The townspeople came with sticks and stones. They were huffing and puffing as they walked around looking for the wolf. Then they asked, "Where's the wolf?"

Nicholas hid his grin and lied, "The wolf ran into the forest when he saw you coming."

Some of the men and women began to wonder about this when they saw the sheep so quiet. "Where did the wolf come from?" asked a man.

Nicholas pointed and said, "Right by that rock."

Some men and women walked to the rock and saw no wolf tracks. One of the women came to him and said, "Let me warn you! If you're playing tricks on us, we will not come to help you!"

His dad also warned him, "Nicholas, I hope you're not lying."

"I'm not lying," Nicholas said.

As the townspeople went away, they began talking among themselves. "There was no wolf," a farmer said. "The sheep are much too quiet. Nicholas is lying."

A woman added, "We also didn't see any wolf tracks."

"I'm not helping him anymore," a farmer said.

"I'm also not helping," a store owner said.

"I don't know," said a woman. "Maybe Nicholas is telling the truth."

Nicholas kept watching the sheep, and day after day he used his slingshot to shoot stones at trees and rocks. "Ohhhhh!" he groaned. "This gets so boring. What else can I do?"

But whenever Nicholas thought about the townspeople running up the hill, slipping and falling, he laughed and laughed. "Ha! Ha! Ha! That was the funniest thing I have ever seen!"

One day Nicholas became so bored, that without thinking, he suddenly jumped on a rock and yelled as loud as he could, "Wolf! Wolf!"

When the townspeople heard, "Wolf! Wolf!" they stopped what they were doing and listened. Many of them said, "That's Nicholas yelling, 'Wolf! Wolf!' He's playing a trick again."

Others said, "We know it's Nicholas, but maybe a wolf is attacking his sheep this time. We're going to help him."

A few townspeople ran up the hill to help Nicholas. As Nicholas watched them run up the hill, he laughed so hard that he had to hold his tummy. "Ha! Ha! Ha! This is so, so funny."

However, this time when the townspeople ran up the hill, they looked around to see if they could find Nicholas. When a woman saw him, she yelled, "Look! I see Nicholas peeking from behind a rock and laughing."

When the townspeople saw him laughing, they were furious. An angry man said, "There's no wolf! We saw you laughing."

A woman asked, "Why did you call us when there was no wolf?"

Seeing that he could no longer hide what he had done, Nicholas said, "I was bored, so I decided to have a little fun."

"It wasn't fun for us!" said a man shaking his finger at him. "Now we know you're a liar and can never be trusted! You'll never see us again!"

Then Mom came and scolded him, "Don't ever do that again! That's lying! When you become known as a liar, how can anyone trust you?"

"I was just having a little fun," whispered Nicholas.

"To you it was fun," Dad said, "but not to the townspeople. They're furious. They stopped what they were doing to help you. To them you're now a liar who can never be trusted. Don't ever do that again!"

But Nicholas was not listening. He was furious. When Dad and Mom left, he kicked a stone and grumbled, "Why is everyone so mad

at me? Can't they take a little joke? I was just having a little fun. And why is everyone talking to me about lying?"

Then one day while watching his sheep,
Nicholas heard a rustling noise coming from the
forest. "I wonder what that is?" he said to himself.

He quickly stopped what he was doing, turned around, and looked into the forest. "What's that I see?" he said trembling.

Suddenly, the hungry wolf ran out of the forest. "Oh, nooooo!" cried Nicholas. "It's the big bad wolf! He's coming to attack my sheep! I need to call for help!"

Nicholas quickly jumped on a rock, waved his hat wildly, and screamed as loud as he could, "Wolf! Wolf! There's really a wolf! I'm not lying! Please! Come and help me save my sheep!"

The hungry wolf dashed towards the sheep. Nicholas kept waving his hat and screaming as loud as he could, "Wolf! Wolf! I'm not lying! A wolf is really attacking my sheep! Please! Come quickly! Help me save my sheep!"

However, when the townspeople heard Nicholas screaming for help, they did not stop working. They just waved their hands and said, "That's Nicholas. He's a liar and can't be trusted. We're not falling for his tricks again."

Nicholas's parents happened to be visiting some friends in the next town, so they did not hear Nicholas crying, "Wolf! Wolf!"

As Nicholas watched the wolf drag his favorite lamb into the forest, he groaned, "Ohhhhh! Why didn't I listen? Why did I lie and act so foolish?"

When Dad and Mom came home and heard what Nicholas had done, they quickly went to see him. When Nicholas saw Dad and Mom coming, he ran to meet them. "I'm so sorry for being foolish and lying," he cried. "I promise. I will never lie again. Please forgive me. Now I see how foolish it is to lie."

Dad and Mom gave him a great big hug and said, "We forgive you."

Nicholas went before the townspeople and said, "I am very, very sorry for lying. Please forgive me. Now I understand how foolish it is to lie. From now on, I will always tell the truth."

"You're forgiven!" the townspeople shouted. After the meeting some townspeople came to him and said, "We're proud of you for having the courage to say, 'I am sorry.'"

True to his word, from that day on Nicholas always told the truth. He then became known as one who could always be trusted.

Books that Motivate Children to Succeed

N 978-1-57537-075-0

ISBN 978-1-57537-079-8

ISBN 978-1-57537-076-7

ISBN 978-1-57537-080-4

N 978-1-57537-081-1

ISBN 978-1-57537-082-8

ISBN 978-1-57537-083-5

ISBN 978-1-57537-084-2

N 978-1-57537-077-4

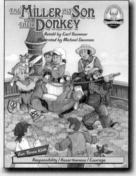

ISBN 978-1-57537-085-9

ISBN 978-1-57537-078-1

ISBN 978-1-57537-086-6

Sommer's Lively Retelling of These Classic Fables

- Androcles and the Lion
- The Boy Who Cried Wolf
- Chicken Little
- The Country Mouse and the City Mouse
- The Emperor's New Clothes
- The Lion and the Mouse

- The Lion and the Three Bulls
- The Little Red Hen
- Little Red Riding Hood
- The Miller, His Son, and Their Donkey
- Stone Soup
- The Tortoise and the Hare

Library Edition: Cloth Reinforced Binding 8 1/4" x 11 1/4"
Set of 12: ISBN 978-1-57537-087-3

Available In Digital Format
www.AdvancePublishing.com